Rae
the Rollercoaster
Fairy

Join the **Rainbow Magic Reading Challenge!**

Read the story and collect your fairy points to climb the

To Freya, with love

Special thanks to
Rachel Elliot

ORCHARD BOOKS

First published in Great Britain in 2018 by The Watts Publishing Group

1 3 5 7 9 10 8 6 4 2

© 2018 Rainbow Magic Limited.
© 2018 HIT Entertainment Limited.
Illustrations © Orchard Books 2018

HIT entertainment

The moral rights of the author and illustrator have been asserted.

A CIP catalogue record for this book is available from the British Library.

ISBN 978 1 40834 963 2

Printed and bound in Great Britain by CPI Group (UK) Ltd, Croydon, CR0 4YY

MIX
Paper from
responsible sources
FSC® C104740

The paper and board used in this book are made from wood from responsible sources

Orchard Books
An imprint of Hachette Children's Group
Part of The Watts Publishing Group Limited
Carmelite House, 50 Victoria Embankment, London EC4Y 0DZ

An Hachette UK Company
www.hachette.co.uk
www.hachettechildrens.co.uk

Rae
the Rollercoaster
Fairy

by Daisy Meadows

ORCHARD

www.rainbowmagic.co.uk

The Fairyland
Palace

Fairyland Funfair

Rachel's
House

TIPPINGTON
TOWN

Jack Frost's Spell

I want a funfair just for me!
(I'll let in goblins, grudgingly.)
With stolen keyrings in my hand,
I'll spoil the fun the fairies planned.

Their rides will stop, their stalls will fail,
Their food will all turn sour and stale.
I'll make the goblins squeal and smirk.
This time my plan is going to work!

Contents

The Fair's in Town!

Rachel Walker cartwheeled her way along the pavement towards her school. She was excited that her best friend Kirsty Tate had come to stay with her. They were on their way to a summer funfair on the playing field at Rachel's school.

"Watch out for the lamppost," called

Kirsty from behind her.

Giggling and panting, Rachel jumped up. She had felt fizzy with fun ever since she had woken up. Today was the opening morning of the funfair, and they

had agreed to get there early so that they could enjoy it for as long as possible.

"This is going to be so much fun," Rachel said. "I just know it."

"Me too," said Kirsty. "But we always have fun together."

"Especially when we're on a fairy adventure," Rachel added, lowering her voice in case anyone was listening.

Since the girls first met on Rainspell Island, they had shared many magical adventures. Their friendship with the fairies was a secret that they had promised to keep for ever.

"Oh my goodness, look," said Rachel, pointing at the trees ahead.

The top of a Ferris wheel was poking up above the branches.

"And look behind it," said Kirsty,

jumping up and down on the spot.
"Rachel, it's a rollercoaster!"

Sure enough, a silvery rollercoaster
track was arching and dipping on the
other side of the Ferris wheel. Rachel felt
a thrilling tingle run through her body.
She looked at Kirsty, knowing that her
best friend was bubbling with the same
excitement.

"Let's run," she said. "Let's get there as
fast as we can."

Giggling, the best friends sprinted along
the pavement, all the time glimpsing
more and more of the funfair through
the trees ahead. Breathlessly, they called
out to each other every time they saw
something new.

"Candyfloss!"

"Dodgems!"

"Helter-skelter!"

Large signs pointed the way towards the entrance, and at last they arrived, their hearts racing. An arched gateway had been set up at the end of the school playing field, and the sign above it was printed in bright, bold lettering: *The Fernandos' Fabulous Funfair.*

The little wooden gate was closed, but on the other side of it they could see a ticket booth with two girls leaning against it. They looked very alike, with long blonde plaits and freckly noses.

"Hello," said Rachel in a friendly voice. "Is this where we buy tickets?"

"We're not quite open yet," said one of the girls with a smile. "But you are first in the queue. Welcome to our funfair."

"Your funfair?" said Kirsty. "Does your family own it?"

"Yes, the girl replied. "I'm Matilda Fernando, and this is my twin Georgia. Our parents run the funfair, and we help out in the school holidays."

"I'm Rachel, and this is my best friend Kirsty," said Rachel. "Wow, it must be so incredible to live in a funfair. I bet you know it really well. Which ride do you like best?"

Matilda and Georgia looked at each other.

"The Zippy Zoom rollercoaster," they said together.

"It's fantastic," said Matilda. "But the queue gets really long, so you should go there first before it gets too crowded."

"Good plan," said Kirsty. "Why don't you both come with us? It would be even more fun to ride the rollercoaster with the owners."

While they had been talking, other people had started to arrive, and now the queue behind them was quite long.

"Matilda, Georgia, we're about to open," said a lady who was walking

towards them from the funfair. She had the same blonde hair and freckled nose as the girls.

"Mum, can we go on the rollercoaster with our new friends?" asked Matilda. "Please?"

Her mum smiled at Rachel and Kirsty and held out her hand.

"Hello, I'm Fifi," she said. "Are you both from here in Tippington?"

"I am," said Rachel. "Kirsty's from Wetherbury, but she's staying with me. I'm Rachel."

"It's nice to meet you, girls," said Fifi. "Now, will you all look after each other on that rollercoaster?"

The four girls nodded eagerly.

"Then have fun," said Fifi.

She opened the gate and Rachel and

Kirsty gave her their entrance money. They each got a purple ticket with a golden trim.

"Don't lose those," said Georgia. "They will let you on to all of the rides at the funfair all day long."

The girls put their tickets away and looked up at the array of rides and stalls in front of them. The rollercoaster was towering above everything.

"Let's hurry to the Zippy Zoom," said Matilda in a happy voice. "Race you!"

The Zippy Zoom

Giggling, the four girls ran through the funfair towards the Zippy Zoom rollercoaster. Rachel and Kirsty showed the man on the gate their tickets and he let them on board, and then waved Georgia and Matilda through.

"As you've never ridden the Zippy Zoom before, you should have the best seats," said Georgia, leading the girls to the front of the rollercoaster.

Kirsty and Rachel climbed into the front seats, and Georgia and Matilda took the seats behind them. More children poured through the gate and soon the rest of the rollercoaster was full.

"We'll set off in a minute," said Matilda. "Hold on tight – the Zippy Zoom really lives up to its name."

Kirsty and Rachel could sense each other's excitement as they pulled down the safety bar.

"My tummy's full of butterflies," said Rachel.

"Mine too," said Kirsty. "I love this feeling."

The rollercoaster gave a little jerk and began to move forwards. The girls waited for it to speed up, but it carried on moving at a snail's pace. It inched up the slope, and the passengers started muttering to each other.

"Something must be wrong," said Georgia. "The Zippy Zoom is usually whizzing along by now. It's meant to be fast and fun, but this is slow and dull."

The rollercoaster crawled on around the track. Instead of squeals and shouts from the other passengers, Rachel and Kirsty could hear disappointed, cross voices.

"I wish we'd never got on this ride."

"I hope the rest of the funfair is more exciting."

They went down a final slope and came to a gentle stop.

"I'm sorry," said Matilda as they all climbed off the ride. "That was really disappointing."

The four girls stepped down and headed towards the Zippy Zoom exit. On the way, Kirsty noticed a small photo stall. The young man behind the counter was calling out to the passengers as they left the ride, but no one was listening to him.

"There's an automatic camera that takes pictures of passengers at the really hair-raising parts of the rollercoaster ride," said Georgia. "Then the passengers can buy photos to remember how much fun they had."

"They sell photo key rings and mugs as well," said Matilda. "There's usually a big crowd around the stall."

No one was buying anything at the moment. All the photos showed very glum passengers.

"Who would want to remember that ride?" said a boy as he stomped past the stall.

"That was boring," said a young woman.

Georgia and Matilda exchanged a worried glance.

"We'd better go and tell our parents that there's a problem with the Zippy Zoom," said Matilda.

Georgia looked at Rachel and Kirsty.

"Don't worry," she said. "The mechanics will sort it out in no time.

While we're gone, you should go and do
the Lucky Dip – it's fun."

"Oh yes, good idea," said Matilda
at once. "Everyone wins a prize at the
Lucky Dip, so you can't lose."

"We'll catch up with you later,"
Georgia promised.

Kirsty and Rachel waved goodbye to
their new friends and then went to find
the Lucky Dip. It was next to the hoopla

LUCKY DIP

stall, and it was a large, red wooden box, decorated with yellow swirling flowers. There was a hole just big enough for a hand, and inside the girls could see exciting-looking shapes wrapped in colourful tissue paper.

"Roll up, roll up!" shouted a man who was standing beside the box. "Everyone's a winner!"

The girls handed over their money, and then took it in turns to reach into the hole and pull out a prize. It was fun to reach in among the knobbly packages and hear the crackling paper. Soon they were each holding a present.

"Let's go and find a quiet place where we can open them," said Rachel.

They ran over to the fence around the playing field and sat down in the long

grass. Rachel ripped her tissue paper
open and found a turquoise pencil case,
dotted with sparkling stars.

"That's lovely," said Kirsty. "I wonder
what I've got."

She looked down at her present
and gasped. The present was
glowing, and both girls had
seen that kind of glow
before.

"Could it be a
fairy?" Kirsty
whispered.

Rachel forgot all
about her pencil case and
crossed her fingers.

"I hope so," she said. "That really would
make today absolutely perfect."

Quickly, Kirsty tore off the tissue paper.

27

There was a flurry of magical sparkles, and then a fairy fluttered out from the tissue paper. She looked up at the girls with shining eyes.

"Hello, Rachel and Kirsty," she said. "I'm Rae the Rollercoaster Fairy."

Fun and Frost

Rae was wearing skinny jeans and a striped T-shirt. Her dark hair was piled up in a loose bun, and her gauzy wings were tinged with blue. Rachel and Kirsty glanced around to check that no one was watching. Lots of people were milling around the funfair, but not a single person was coming their way. The girls smiled at Rae.

"It's great to meet you," said Kirsty.

"Thank goodness you're here," added Rachel. "We've just been on the Zippy Zoom rollercoaster, and it was really slow. It wasn't fun at all."

"There's a good reason for that," said

Rae in a serious voice. "My magical key ring has been stolen. Rachel and Kirsty, please will you come with me to Fairyland? I really need your help."

"Of course we will," said Kirsty, and Rachel nodded.

Rae raised her wand and a fountain of sparkling fairy dust erupted from the tip. It swirled around the girls, and they felt their skin tingling as they magically shrank to fairy size. Delicate wings unfurled on their backs, and they

fluttered into the air beside Rae. She smiled at them and spoke the words of a spell.

"Hold on tight, for I have planned
A magic ride to Fairyland.
Fun has faded, rides are slow.
I need your help to make them go!"

Rachel and Kirsty heard the sound of far-off silver bells. Then, faster than a speeding rollercoaster, the green playing field disappeared and they were blinking in the Fairyland sunshine.

"Why can I still hear the funfair?" said Rachel.

"Because that's not the Tippington funfair," said Rae, smiling. "That's the Fairyland Summer Fair."

Kirsty and Rachel looked around in wonder. They were standing outside the

Fairyland Palace, and it looked very different. A rollercoaster track wound over the roof and around the turrets. Dodgems whizzed around the grounds and there were food and games stalls in every nook and cranny.

"This is incredible," said Kirsty. "Did

you create all this, Rae?"

"Not just me," said Rae. "Let me introduce you to the other Funfair Fairies."

Three other fairies came fluttering towards them.

"Meet Fatima the Face-Painting Fairy, Paloma the Dodgems Fairy and Bobbi

the Bouncy Castle Fairy," said Rae.

All the Funfair Fairies waved at them, but they looked very glum.

"Thank you both for coming," said Fatima. "We were hoping you'd help us. The king and queen are waiting for you. They'll explain everything."

The fairies took their hands and

led them to the glassy Seeing Pool.
King Oberon and Queen Titania were
standing beside it, and Rachel and Kirsty
curtsied.

"Welcome to Fairyland," said the queen
in a calm voice. "Thank you for coming.
We can always rely on you to help us."

"What's happened?" asked Rachel.

"Jack Frost happened," said King
Oberon. "He stole the Funfair Fairies'
magical key rings."

"The Fairyland Summer Fair is
opening tomorrow evening," said Queen
Titania. "If the Funfair Fairies don't get
their key rings back before then, funfairs
everywhere will be a disaster. Let me
show you what Jack Frost did."

She waved her wand over the Seeing
Pool, and the surface rippled. Then a

picture appeared on the water, just as if
they were watching a film.

"The fairies were just finishing building
the funfair when Jack Frost sneaked in,"
said King Oberon.

They watched as the Funfair
Fairies created stalls and rides.
Nearby, Kylie the Carnival Fairy and
Layla the Candyfloss Fairy were waving
their wands to add new games and

activities. There was a flash of green in the background and four goblins tiptoed forwards – one behind each of the Funfair Fairies. They stretched out their bony fingers and stole a key ring from the pocket of each fairy.

Rae turned and cried out in alarm. But at that moment Jack Frost appeared in a flash of lightning. The goblins scurried behind him, sniggering.

"I'm going to

build the biggest, best funfair ever, right in the middle of my Ice Castle," said Jack Frost, cackling. "With your magical key rings, I will be the owner of the only fun funfair anywhere."

There was a bolt of icy blue magic, and Jack Frost and the goblins disappeared. Kirsty and Rachel exchanged a worried glance.

"Until the magical key rings are back where they belong, none of the rides and games at funfairs will be any fun," said Queen Titania.

"The Fairyland Summer Fair will be ruined," said Kirsty.

"And so will the funfair in Tippington," said Rachel. "We have to stop Jack Frost and get the magical key rings back."

Queen Titania gazed into the Seeing

Pool once again.

"My magic tells me that he has left Fairyland," she said. "Rae, I think you should take Kirsty and Rachel back home. We must keep the human world safe."

Kirsty and Rachel curtsied again.

"We'll stop him, Your Majesty," Kirsty promised.

The king and queen nodded, and Rae waved her wand. In a glittering whirl of fairy dust, the girls found themselves human size again, back beside the playing-field fence in Tippington. The sounds of Fernandos' Fabulous Funfair drifted over to them. Rae slipped into Rachel's pocket.

"Let's find Jack Frost," said Rachel.

A Bumpy Ride

There was a long queue at the Zippy Zoom rollercoaster. Kirsty looked up and tugged on Rachel's arm.

"The rollercoaster's working," she said. "Why is it going so fast all of a sudden?"

Both girls stared as the Zippy Zoom raced around the track. It climbed and dived and looped the loop.

"Something about the rollercoaster looks wrong," said Rachel.

"It looks empty," said Kirsty. "Is anyone actually riding it?"

Just then they heard their names being called. Georgia was running towards them.

"She looks worried," said Rachel, waving to her.

Georgia reached them and stopped to catch her breath.

"Something has gone wrong," she said, panting. "There are only four boys on the rollercoaster, but it's zooming

around and around and not stopping to
let other passengers on."

"Oh my goodness," said Kirsty, her
thoughts racing. "Those boys must be
scared."

"That's the weird thing," said Georgia.
"They seem to be enjoying it. Maybe
they don't understand that there's a
problem. They're cackling with laughter,
even though they are starting to look a
bit green."

Rachel and Kirsty glanced at each
other in alarm. Whenever they heard
that someone looked green, it made them
think of goblins.

"I have to find my parents," said
Georgia. "They'll want to know about
this."

She ran off, and at that moment the

girls spotted Matilda. She was talking to a man in red overalls and the girls hurried over to her.

"I can't understand it," the man was saying. "First the rollercoaster was too slow and now it's too fast. But I can't find anything wrong with it."

"This is Jake," said Matilda. "He's one of the funfair mechanics. We were hoping that he'd know what's going on."

Kirsty and Rachel exchanged another worried glance. They had just heard that the boys on the ride looked green, and now the mechanic couldn't work out what was wrong. Kirsty said what they were both thinking.

"Could those be goblins on the rollercoaster, instead of boys?" she asked in a low voice.

The girls felt sure that Rae must be
wondering the same thing.

"I know how we
can find out," said
Rachel. "Let's
turn into fairies
and fly up to the
rollercoaster."

"Find a place
to hide," whispered
Rae from inside
her pocket.

The girls ducked down behind the
rollercoaster track and Rae fluttered
out of the pocket. With a flick of her
wand, she turned Rachel and Kirsty
into fairies again. Then all three of
them shot upwards and hovered over the
rollercoaster.

The Zippy Zoom was climbing up a
steep slope, with four figures squeezed
into the front car. They had green
faces and long noses, and they were all
wearing bright-green shorts and T-shirts.

"Goblins," said Kirsty. "I knew it."

"Look at that goblin at the front," said
Rachel. "He's holding a key ring – is it
yours, Rae?"

"Yes!" said Rae in delight.

She darted towards the goblin,
but before she could reach him, the
rollercoaster started to speed down the
steep slope again. The goblins became a
green blur as they zoomed past.

"We have to get inside the
rollercoaster," said Kirsty. "Are you ready?
One ... two ... three ... go."

The three fairies zipped into the

rollercoaster car with the goblins and held on to the safety bar.

"This is going to be a bumpy ride," cried Rae.

The goblins saw the fairies and let out shrieks of dismay.

"Fairies!" squealed the smallest goblin, who was squashed into the corner. "Get off our rollercoaster and buzz off!"

The goblin holding the key ring gave
an alarmed squawk.

"Faster!" he shouted at the key ring,
and the rollercoaster sped up.

"I'm getting really dizzy," said the
smallest goblin, closing his eyes and
smiling. "I love it."

"Me too," said the goblin with the key ring. "This is so much fun!"

The third and fourth goblins were clinging to each other, giggling hysterically.

"Stop the ride!" Rachel called out. "The rollercoaster is meant for everyone to have fun on – not just you."

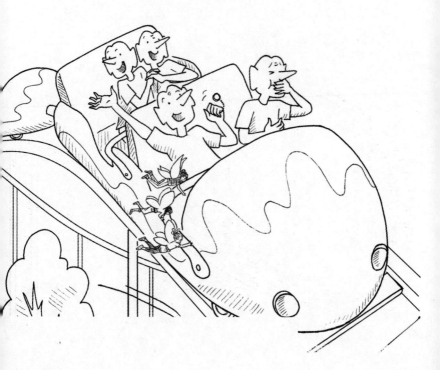

"Guess what?" said the third goblin in a mocking, sing-song voice. "We don't care. We're going to ride this rollercoaster for as long as we want."

"And there's nothing you can do about it," added the fourth goblin as the rollercoaster zoomed along the track. "Woo-hoo!"

Picture Perfect

The Zippy Zoom hurtled down another
slope and the goblins squealed with
dizziness and delight. The fairies were
thrown to the floor, and they clung
to each other, keeping away from the
goblins' enormous feet.

"I've got an idea," shouted Kirsty over
the rattling noise. "Can we make the

rollercoaster go faster? If we can make
the goblins get even dizzier, maybe we'll
be able to grab the key ring from the
goblin in the front."

Rae nodded and beckoned to Rachel
and Kirsty. They all flew out and
swooped around the rollercoaster.

"Let's get away from them!" shrieked
the fourth goblin.

The goblin with the key ring held it up
in front of him, and the rollercoaster went
even faster.

"The goblins are going even greener,"
said Rachel.

She put on an extra burst of speed and
reached out for the magical key ring. But
just then the goblin tucked it under his
bottom.

"How are we going to get it back
now?" cried Rae.

Suddenly, Rachel remembered the
photo key rings on the stall on the way
out of the rollercoaster ride.

"I've got an idea," she said, clasping
Kirsty and Rae by their hands. "Rae,
you'll need to turn us back into humans."

The three fairies fluttered down behind
the rollercoaster, and Rae returned
Rachel and Kirsty to human size. Rae
slipped into Rachel's pocket again.

The girls came out from behind the

rollercoaster and made their way towards
the photo stall they had seen earlier.
Matilda and Georgia were standing
beside it, looking upset.

"I can't find my parents anywhere,"
said Georgia. "Jake has gone to look at
the controls again. Until we can stop
the rollercoaster, no one else can have a
turn."

"Could I see the picture of the boys taken by the automatic camera?" Rachel asked.

She looked around for the young man who had been working in the photo stall earlier.

"Olly's taking a break," said Matilda. "But I know how to work the camera."

She slipped behind the stall and tapped on the computer. A photo of the goblins popped up on the screen.

"Goodness, they look very green," said Georgia. "They must be feeling really sick, poor things."

"Maybe it's just a trick of the light," said Rachel quickly. "They're smiling and laughing, see?"

"It's a really happy picture," said Kirsty. "I love seeing friends having fun together.

Could I buy the photo on a key ring?"

"Sure," said Matilda. "But you don't have to buy it. Let it be a present to say sorry for the boring rollercoaster ride you had."

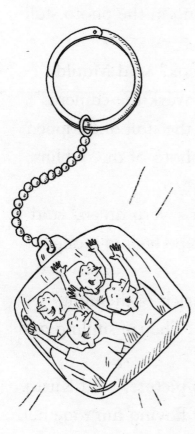

She tapped a few buttons and then a tiny photo popped out of the printer. Matilda clicked it into a key ring and handed it to Kirsty. At that moment, Georgia gave an exclamation.

"I can see Mum and Dad," she

said. "Come on, Matilda, let's go and tell them what's been going on."

The sisters ran off and Kirsty showed Rachel the photo key ring.

"It's a great photo," said Rachel. "Fingers crossed the goblins like it."

The friends exchanged a hopeful glance.

"Quickly, hide again, so I can turn you into fairies," whispered Rae from Kirsty's bag.

The girls ran behind the rollercoaster and Rae waved her wand. Rachel and Kirsty shrank to fairy size and fluttered into the air. They carried the photo key ring between them, because it had stayed the same size.

"Now we just have to catch the rollercoaster," said Rae with a smile.

"Time for some fast flying!"

They raced after the rollercoaster,
dipping and diving around the track.
Kirsty saw Rachel's wings moving so fast
they were just blurs, and she knew that
her wings must be the same.

"Just ... a little ... faster ..." Rae said,

panting with the effort.

They put on another burst of speed and managed to perch on the safety bar inside the rollercoaster car. Rachel and Kirsty held up the photo key ring between them.

"Look," said Kirsty. "It's all of you."

The goblins leaned forwards to look, but the rollercoaster car was shaking so much that they couldn't see it.

"I want to see my photo," squawked the smallest goblin. "Slow this rollercoaster down!"

Magical Mementos

The goblin at the front brought out Rae's magical key ring and whispered, "Slow down," to it. The rollercoaster slowed down until it was crawling along. The goblins giggled at the photo.

"We look funny," said the third goblin.

"Speak for yourself," said the fourth. "I

look handsome."

The third goblin elbowed him in the ribs and he squawked.

"It's a great way to remember the fun you've had on here," said Rachel. "We'll give it to you if you will give us Rae's magical key ring."

The goblins looked at each other.

"Jack Frost told us to keep hold of this," said the goblin holding Rae's key ring.

"It's been fun," said the smallest goblin. "But I'm tired of feeling dizzy now. I've had enough of this ride."

The three other goblins looked at each other and nodded. Then the goblin at the front held out his hand with the magical key ring on his palm. Smiling, Rae fluttered forwards and landed on his hand as lightly as a feather. She bent down to

touch the key
ring, and it
instantly
shrank to
fairy size.

Kirsty
and
Rachel let
the photo key
ring drop gently
into the goblin's hand, and all the
goblins leaned over to see their picture.
The fairies fluttered upwards as the
rollercoaster stopped at the bottom of the
track. The ride was over at last.

The goblins climbed out of the carriage
on wobbly legs. They clung to each other
as they staggered off, giggling at their
funny photo key ring. Rachel, Kirsty

and Rae perched on the frame, keeping
high up so they were out of sight. They
watched as a queue of people climbed on
board the Zippy Zoom. As soon as it was
full, the rollercoaster zoomed away – not
too fast and not slow.

"It looks like really good fun," said

Kirsty. "I can't wait to try it out."

"That's exactly what you should do," said Rae. "You deserve a wonderful rollercoaster ride after helping me so much. Thank you for everything you did. I'd never have got my magical key ring back without you."

"Are you going back to Fairyland?"

Rachel asked.

"Yes," said Rae. "Now that I have my magic key ring back, I can sort out the rollercoaster at the Summer Fair in Fairyland. I can make sure that everyone will have fun there as well as here."

Rachel and Kirsty hugged Rae, and then they all fluttered down to land on the grass behind the rollercoaster. With a

flick of Rae's wand, Rachel and Kirsty
were human again. They waved at the
little fairy, and she blew a kiss at them.
Then there was a burst of sparkling fairy
dust, and Rae had disappeared. Rachel
and Kirsty exchanged a happy smile.

"If we hurry
we'll get on the
next ride of the
Zippy Zoom," said
Kirsty. "Race you!"

Half an hour
later, Rachel and
Kirsty stepped off
the Zippy Zoom,
holding hands and
giggling.

"My legs feel
all wobbly," said

Rachel. "Georgia and Matilda were right
– that was the best fun."

They went to the photo stall, where
they found Matilda and Georgia waiting
for them.

"There are some great shots of you

two," said Matilda, beaming with pleasure. "Come and see."

The girls giggled as they looked through the funny photos. They had shrieked and laughed all the way around the rollercoaster track.

"I'm glad it's working again," said Georgia. "We have no idea how, though. Jake says he didn't mend anything. It's almost as if it fixed itself – like magic."

Rachel and Kirsty smiled at each other. They couldn't tell the Fernando sisters that it was fairy magic.

"I'd love to buy a key ring as a memento," said Kirsty.

"Me too," said Rachel, smiling at her best friend. "It's the perfect way to remember our adventure."

They chose pictures that showed them

laughing together, and put the finished key rings into their pockets.

"There's so much more for you to see at the funfair," said Matilda. "I wish we could show you around, but Georgia and I have a few chores to do for our parents."

"We can't wait to explore the rest of

the fair," said Kirsty.

"I'm sure we'll see you later," Rachel added.

"Have fun," called Matilda as she hurried off with her sister.

Rachel and Kirsty waved goodbye, and then exchanged a worried glance.

"We still have three more magical key

rings to find for the Funfair Fairies," Rachel said. "Without them, everything at the funfair will keep going wrong. Do you think we can do it, Kirsty? Can we defeat Jack Frost's plans again?"

Kirsty linked arms with her best friend. "Of course we can," she said. "We have magic and friendship on our side, and that means Jack Frost can never win. Together, we can give every adventure a happy ending!"

The End

Now it's time for Kirsty and Rachel to help...

Fatima the Face-Painting Fairy

Read on for a sneak peek...

Kirsty Tate popped the last, scrumptious bite of hot dog into her mouth and licked her fingers. Her best friend, Rachel Walker, had already finished her burger. She was pulling funny faces in the silly mirrors outside the funhouse.

"I love these," said Rachel, pulling her ears out so they looked huge and wobbly in the mirror. "I think they might be my favourite thing at the funfair."

"You've said that about everything so far," said Kirsty, giggling.

The girls were spending the day at The Fernandos' Fabulous Funfair. It had come to the playing field of Rachel's school in Tippington, and Kirsty was visiting for the weekend so that they could enjoy it together.

"The Zippy Zoom rollercoaster was lots of fun," said Kirsty, coming to stand beside Rachel in front of the first mirror.

"So was the Lucky Dip," said Rachel, moving on to the second mirror. "And it was great to make some new friends."

Matilda and Georgia Fernando were twin sisters whose parents ran the funfair. The girls had met them when they arrived, and they had got on instantly.

"I look hilarious," said Kirsty, staring at herself in the first mirror. "I'm just like a beanpole. "

She bent her knees and bobbed up and down, giggling as her reflection grew tall and bendy.

"Come and see this one," said Rachel, chuckling at herself looking as round as a beach ball, with a tiny head.

The girls laughed as they moved along the row of mirrors, changing shape in each one. But when they reached the last mirror, their reflections seemed normal.

"What's funny about this one?" said Rachel.

The girls stared at themselves, and then Kirsty saw it.

"Look at our feet," she said, bursting with laughter.

Their feet looked enormous, as if they were wearing clown shoes.

"That's brilliant," said Rachel, lifting one foot after the other and waggling them around.

But then Kirsty spotted something in the mirror that made her forget all about her huge feet. Spinning around, she grabbed Rachel's arm and pointed at a boy walking through the crowd.

"Can you see what I see?" she asked her best friend. "Is that ... can that possibly be Jack Frost?"

Rachel gaped at the boy. He had a blue face and a beard that made him look exactly like the fairies' worst enemy.

"He can't be," said Rachel. "He's too short, and look at his feet – they're tiny."

Read **Fatima the Face-Painting Fairy** to find out what adventures are in store for Kirsty and Rachel!

RAINBOW magic

Calling all parents, carers and teachers!
The Rainbow Magic fairies are here to help
your child enter the magical world of reading.
Whatever reading stage they are at, there's
a Rainbow Magic book for everyone!
Here is Lydia the Reading Fairy's guide to
supporting your child's journey at all levels.

Starting Out

(1) Our Rainbow Magic Beginner Readers are perfect for first-time readers who are just beginning to develop reading skills and confidence. Approved by teachers, they contain a full range of educational levelling, as well as lively full-colour illustrations.

Developing Readers

(2) Rainbow Magic Early Readers contain longer stories and wider vocabulary for building stamina and growing confidence. These are adaptations of our most popular Rainbow Magic stories, specially developed for younger readers in conjunction with an Early Years reading consultant, with full-colour illustrations.

Going Solo

(3) The Rainbow Magic chapter books – a mixture of series and one-off specials – contain accessible writing to encourage your child to venture into reading independently. These highly collectible and much-loved magical stories inspire a love of reading to last a lifetime.

www.rainbowmagicbooks.co.uk

"Rainbow Magic got my daughter reading chapter books. Great sparkly covers, cute fairies and traditional stories full of magic that she found impossible to put down" - Mother of Edie (6 years)

"Florence LOVES the Rainbow Magic books. She really enjoys reading now" - Mother of Florence (6 years)

The Rainbow Magic
Reading Challenge

Well done, fairy friend – you have completed the book!
This book was worth 5 points.

See how far you have climbed on the
Reading Rainbow opposite.

The more books you read, the more points you will get,
and the closer you will be to becoming a Fairy Princess!

How to get your Reading Rainbow
1. Cut out the coin below
2. Go to the Rainbow Magic website
3. Download and print out your poster
4. Add your coin and climb up the Reading Rainbow!

There's all this and lots more at
www.rainbowmagicbooks.co.uk

You'll find activities, competitions, stories, a special
newsletter and complete profiles of all the
Rainbow Magic fairies. Find a fairy with your name!